This Topsy and Tim book belongs to

ZARA

With thanks to the charity Community Hygiene Concern
for their helpful advice.
Help Line: 020 7686 4321
Website: http://www.chc.org/bugbusting

Published by Ladybird Books Ltd
80 Strand London WC2R ORL
A Penguin Company

1 3 5 7 9 10 8 6 4 2

Printed in Italy

Have Itchy
Heads

Jean and **Gareth Adamson**

Topsy and Tim had itchy heads,
but nobody noticed them scratching.
Mummy didn't notice and Dad
didn't notice.

Then, one Friday afternoon, Topsy
and Tim came running out of school
with a letter for Mummy and Dad.
All the other children had letters too.
The letter said: "Dear Parents,
There is an outbreak of head lice at
school. Please check your child's hair.
The enclosed leaflet will explain
what to look for."

Mummy showed the letter to Dad.
"Topsy and Tim can't possibly have
head lice," said Mummy. "We often
shampoo their hair."

"Head lice love clean hair," said Topsy.
"Miss Terry said so."

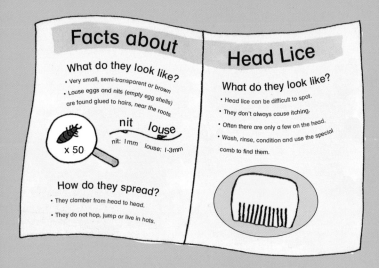

Facts about

What do they look like?

• Very small, semi-transparent or brown
• Louse eggs and nits (empty egg shells) are found glued to hairs, near the roots

nit   louse

x 50

nit: 1mm   louse: 1-3mm

How do they spread?

• They clamber from head to head.
• They do not hop, jump or live in hats.

Head Lice

What do they look like?

• Head lice can be difficult to spot.
• They don't always cause itching.
• Often there are only a few on the head.
• Wash, rinse, condition and use the special comb to find them.

Dad read the leaflet carefully. It said all sorts of interesting things about head lice. "It makes me feel itchy to think about it," said Dad, scratching his head.

That night, at bath time, Mummy had a good look in Topsy's hair – and she couldn't believe what she found.

"Come quickly!" she yelled to Dad.
Dad came running to see what
was wrong.
"Topsy has got nits!" said Mummy.
"Have I got nits?" asked Tim.
Dad looked in Tim's hair.
"Tim's got nits too," he said.

It was too late to do anything about it that night, but early the next morning Dad hurried to the chemist's.
"We need something to get rid of head lice," he said.
"Try this bottle of special lotion. I've sold a lot lately," said the chemist.

As soon as Dad got home Mummy
rubbed the lotion on to Topsy's hair
and Dad did Tim's. They had to be
careful not to get it in their eyes.

Then Topsy and Tim played in the garden and let the breeze dry their hair. They were both glad when it was time to wash the lotion off.

On Sunday, Louise Lewis came to play with Topsy and Tim. Mummy saw them with their heads close together.

"Oh dear," she thought. "If Louise has got head lice, Topsy and Tim could catch them again."

On Monday morning, on the way to
school, Topsy and Tim met Tony Welch.
"We had nits in our hair," said Topsy.

"I've had nits three times," said Tony.

Josie Miller helped Topsy and Tim hang their coats up in the cloakroom.
"We had head lice lotion on our hair," Tim told her. "It smelled awful."
"I don't use that lotion because I've got asthma," said Josie.

Topsy and Tim told Miss Terry about
their nits and the head lice lotion.
"I'm glad you got rid of those naughty
creepy crawlies," said Miss Terry.
"I've got some nice little mini-beasts for
you to look at today."

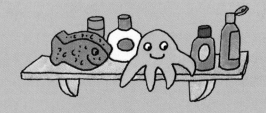

"You look very happy," said Dad
when they got back home.
"We are," said Topsy. "We've found
a good way to get rid of naughty nits."
"No more itchy heads!" said Tim.
"Let's hope so!" said Dad.

"You need to get a special comb like Kerry's for Topsy," said Kerry's mum. "Check her hair with the fine-toothed comb while it's wet and that way you will catch any baby lice as they hatch."

Mummy helped Topsy and Tim and
Kerry to dry their hair.
"This is like being at the hairdressers,"
said Topsy.
"Come and have some lemonade
and biscuits," called Kerry's mum
from the kitchen.

She combed three little lice out and kept on combing but there were no more.

Kerry's mum washed and combed Tim's and Kerry's hair too, just in case.
There were no creepy crawlies in Tim's or Kerry's hair.

Then Kerry's mum combed Topsy's hair, while it was still wet, with a special little fine-toothed comb. "I'm combing Topsy's hair from the roots, very carefully, all over," said Kerry's mum.

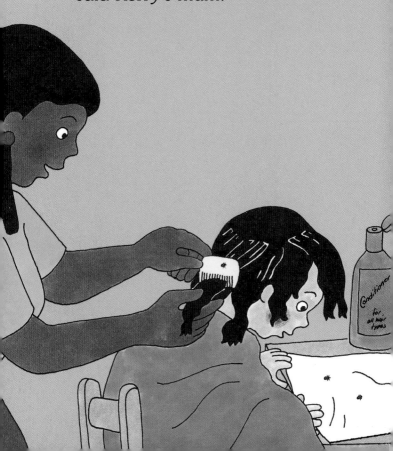

Soon they were all squeezed into Kerry's bathroom. Mummy and Tim and Kerry sat in a row on the edge of the bath and watched what Kerry's mum did.

First she washed Topsy's hair with ordinary shampoo and squirted lots of conditioner on it.

"What's wrong with Topsy?" asked Kerry.
"Topsy's got head lice again and she
hates the smelly lotion," said Tim.
"You don't have to use that lotion to get rid
of them," said Kerry's mum.
"Come home with us and we'll show
you what we do."

At home time Miss Terry told Mummy
about the head louse on Topsy's hair.
Mummy was very upset and Topsy
began to cry.

When Tim was tired of looking at the mini-beasts he looked at Topsy's head with his magnifying glass.
"I can see a mini-beast on Topsy's hair!" he said. Miss Terry came to look.
"Oh dear, Topsy," she said. "I'm afraid it's a head louse."

The nice mini-beasts were all in jam jars on Miss Terry's table. There were ladybirds, woodlice, snails and caterpillars. The children looked at them with magnifying glasses.
It was very interesting.